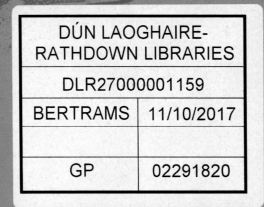

This Faber book belongs to

....

For Leah, Emma and Tom.
Thank you all for your encouragement!
Love C.R.

First published in the UK in 2017
by Faber and Faber Ltd,
Bloomsbury House,
74–77 Great Russell Street,
London WC1B 3DA

The text was first published as the
poem 'Silver' in Walter de la Mare's
Peacock Pie poetry collection in 1913.

Printed in China

Text © The Literary Trustees of
Walter de la Mare, 1969
Illustrations © Carolina Rabei, 2017

A CIP record for this book is available
from the British Library

ISBN 978-0-571-31470-6

10 9 8 7 6 5 4 3 2 1

Silver

Walter de la Mare

Illustrated by Carolina Rabei

ff

FABER & FABER

Slowly, silently,
now the moon

Walks the night
in her silver shoon;

This way, and that,

she peers, and sees

Silver fruit upon silver trees;

One by one the casements catch
Her beams beneath the silvery thatch;

Couched in his kennel, like a log,
With paws of silver sleeps the dog;

From their shadowy cote the white breasts peep
Of doves in a silver-feathered sleep;

A harvest mouse goes
scampering by,

With silver claws,
and silver eye;

And moveless fish
in the water gleam,

By silver reeds in a silver stream.